Horsey Trails

A SUMATRA STORY

By Sibley Miller

Illustrated by Tara Larsen Chang and Jo Gershman

Feiwel and Friends

For everyone at the Children's Garden Preschool.
—Sibley Miller

For Jeff, Maren, and Reilly—thanks for
ongoing support and consolation.
—Tara Larsen Chang

For Debbie, Rachel, Janie, and Julie with love
for all the years of deep friendship.
—Jo Gershman

A FEIWEL AND FRIENDS BOOK
An Imprint of Macmillan

WIND DANCERS: HORSEY TRAILS. Copyright © 2011
by Reeves International, Inc. All rights reserved. Distributed in Canada
by H.B. Fenn and Company, Ltd. BREYER,
WIND DANCERS, and BREYER logos are trademarks and/or registered
trademarks of Reeves International, Inc. Printed in February 2011 in China
by Leo Paper, Heshan City, Guangdong Province.
For information, address Feiwel and Friends,
175 Fifth Avenue, New York, N.Y. 10010.

Library of Congress Cataloging-in-Publication Data

Miller, Sibley.
Horsey trails : a Sumatra story / by Sibley Miller ; illustrated by
Tara Larsen Chang and Jo Gershman.
p. cm. — (Wind Dancers ; #11)
Summary: Four tiny magical horses known as the Wind
Dancers accompany Leanna to horse camp for a week.
ISBN: 978-0-312-60544-5
[1. Horses—Fiction. 2. Magic—Fiction. 3. Camps—Fiction.]
I. Chang, Tara Larsen, ill. II. Gershman, Jo, ill. III. Title. IV. Series.
PZ7.M63373How 2011 [Fic]—dc22 2010037659

Series editor, Susan Bishansky
Designed by Barbara Grzeslo
Feiwel and Friends logo designed by Filomena Tuosto

First Edition: 2011

1 3 5 7 9 10 8 6 4 2

www.feiwelandfriends.com

CONTENTS

Willow Lake Horse Camp

Meet the Wind Dancers

One day, a lonely little girl named Leanna blows on a doozy of a dandelion. To her delight and surprise, four tiny horses spring from the puff of the dandelion seeds!

Four tiny horses with shiny manes and shimmery wings. Four magical horses who can fly!

Dancing on the wind, surrounded by magic halos, they are the Wind Dancers.

The leader of the quartet is **Kona**. She has a violet-black coat and a vivid purple mane, and she flies inside a halo of magical flowers.

Brisa is as pretty as a tropical sunset with her coral-pink color and blonde mane and tail. Magical jewels make up Brisa's halo, and she likes to admire her gems (and herself) every time she looks in a mirror.

Sumatra is silvery blue with sea-green wings. Much like the ocean, she can shift from calm to stormy in a hurry! Her magical halo is made up of ribbons, which flutter and dance as she flies.

The fourth Wind Dancer is—surprise!—a colt. His name is Sirocco. He's a fiery gold, and he likes to go-go-go. Everywhere he goes, his magical halo of butterflies goes, too.

The tiny flying horses live together in the dandelion meadow in a lovely house carved out of the trunk of an apple tree. Every day, Leanna wishes she'll see the magical little horses again. (She's sure they're nearby, but she doesn't know they're invisible to people.) And the Wind Dancers get ready for their next adventure.

CHAPTER 1
Fly Away Home

One summer morning, as they flew across the dandelion meadow, the tiny Wind Dancers were especially bubbly.

Kona whinnied happily as she pranced through the sunny air.

Sirocco played a mischievous game of tag with the tiny butterflies in his magic halo.

And Brisa tossed her well-groomed, blonde mane with extra energy.

Why? Because Sumatra had just sung:

"We're going to see *Leanna*. We're going to see Le-*an-na*!"

Being near the girl who had brought the Wind Dancers to life with just one puff on a dandelion always made the magical little horses happy. Today was no different—until the four friends landed on the windowsill of Leanna's room.

Then their faces fell.

"What—what's this?" Brisa gasped.

"A big mess is what it is!" Sirocco exclaimed. Normally Sirocco liked all things messy, but he knew Leanna, and she was a neat-as-a-freshly-combed-mane sort of girl. So he knew that *something* was up!

"There are shorts and T-shirts and riding breeches everywhere!" Sumatra agreed. "And what are all those tubes and bottles?"

Kona flew in for a closer look.

"Shampoo, sunscreen, bug spray, and a travel-size tube of toothpaste," she reported.

The Wind Dancers also spotted a small pink diary and stationery with stamped, addressed envelopes.

And all of this stuff was piled around a big, army-green duffel bag.

"Leanna's going away!" Brisa exclaimed.

"Where to?" Sumatra gasped.

Before the horses could speculate, Leanna herself tromped into the room with her little sister, Sara, on her heels. One of Leanna's hands was hidden inside a tall black riding boot. With her other hand, she was polishing the boot's shiny leather with a soft cloth.

Leanna plunked the boot on the floor next

to the trunk and tossed her sister a permanent marker.

"Help me out, won't you?" she said. "Mom wrote my name in most of my clothes already, but there are a few extra things I have to pack before tomorrow. *Everything* has to be labeled!"

"Why should I help you," Sara began, jutting out her lower lip, "when you're about to leave me for a week at horse camp? It's no fair!"

The Wind Dancers gasped and gazed at each other.

"Horse camp!" Brisa breathed.

"Wait a minute," Sumatra replied. "A sleep-away camp with horses? That's like a dream come true!"

"Especially for Leanna. She thinks horses are the best!" Sirocco crowed. "Because we are, of course."

Kona laughed at Sirocco, but a moment later, her brow furrowed with worry.

"Horse camp *sounds* exciting," she said, "but won't Leanna miss her family while she's away?"

"*We'll* miss her!" Brisa lamented. "A whole week without Leanna to visit? Whatever will we *do*?"

Sirocco rolled his eyes.

"Sure, we'll miss Leanna, but we'll still have *plenty* to do," he scoffed. "We'll have adventures and make appley treats and 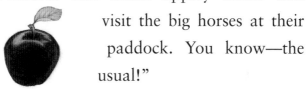 visit the big horses at their paddock. You know—the usual!"

"The usual," Sumatra murmured with a frown. "The usual is so . . . usual. Do you know what would be *un*usual?"

"What?" Brisa said, blinking her pretty, wide eyes.

"Horse camp!" Sumatra whinnied. "Why don't we go with Leanna?"

"But, but," Sirocco stammered, "we don't know *where* this camp is. It could be very far away!"

"What does it matter?" Sumatra responded.

"We'll just hitch a ride with Leanna the way we did when we went to the county fair. It'll be easy!"

"And what about our apple tree house?" Kona said nervously. "If we leave it for a week, it'll get very dusty. Or worse! Some squirrel or chipmunk might think we've abandoned it and move right in!"

"Horse camp sounds awfully . . . rustic to me," Brisa said, eying Leanna's tubes of bug repellent and sunscreen. "What about my beauty routine? Do they even have *mirrors* there?"

"I don't know!" Sumatra replied, her eyes gleaming. "We don't know *anything* about horse camp. That's what makes it so exciting!"

"Or crazy," Kona offered, "depending on how you look at it."

"*Hello?*" Sumatra scoffed. "Remember, this is *horse* camp we're talking about. We'll feel right at home there!"

"Home *away* from home," Sirocco corrected her.

"If that's not an adventure," Sumatra responded coaxingly, "I don't know what is! Come on. I'll even make us all backpack out of my magic ribbons!"

"Well, there *will* be other horses

show us the ropes," Kona said. "Or I guess I should say the *reins*."

"And I suppose I *could* pop a few of my magic jewels onto a cabin wall to serve as mirrors," Brisa said, casting an affectionate glance at the halo of rainbow-colored gems that bobbed around her.

"And I bet my sleep buddy, Jeepers, would like to come along," Sirocco said, shuffling his hooves as he thought about his plush froggie.

"Of course!" Sumatra said. "Leanna's bringing *her* favorite things to camp."

She pointed with her nose at their friend's pink diary and a small pile of model horses.

"I'm going to bring *my* favorite things as well,"

Sumatra added, doling out nose nuzzles to the other Wind Dancers. "My friends!"

"Okay," Kona said with a grin. "You win! Let's go pack."

"Pack!" Brisa whinnied, leaping off Leanna's windowsill and hovering in the air. "It's going to take me all afternoon to gather up my beauty supplies in time to leave tomorrow."

"Not to mention some snacks!" Sirocco said, launching himself toward the Wind Dancers' home.

"And our courage," Kona added, flying after her friends.

"Don't worry," Sumatra called. "Once we get to horse camp, you won't even *think* about home!"

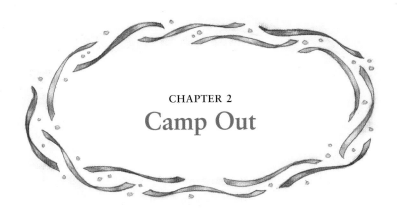

CHAPTER 2
Camp Out

By the time the Wind Dancers arrived at horse camp, *home* was *all* Sumatra could think about!

To start with, the magical horses had hitched a ride in the back of Leanna's family's pickup truck. The drive to the camp—nestled in a green valley surrounded by tree-covered mountains—had been long and winding. Sumatra had gotten a little carsick!

Then the horses—wearing their ribbony new backpacks—had followed Leanna and her family as they toured the camp.

Their first stop had been Leanna's cabin. Instead of walls, the place was sided with huge screens! You could hear every bird chirp, cicada trill, and squirrel-skitter through them.

I wonder how anyone gets any sleep with all that noise, Sumatra had mused, picturing her cozy, quiet sleeping stall in the Wind Dancers' apple tree house.

Next they had gone to the dining hall, where the clatter of children's voices, a hundred forks scraping plates, and all the strange food smells gave Sumatra a headache!

After that, the group had checked out the pasture.

Where are all the dandelions!? Sumatra wondered.

And the arts and crafts cabin.

You can't make pottery with hooves, Sumatra realized sadly.

The lake.

I can't swim!

And finally, the stable, which seemed about a mile long. There were so many big horses in the endless row of stalls, that Sumatra felt too overwhelmed to introduce herself to any one.

After that, the Wind Dancers followed Leanna and her family back to the cabin. The tiny horses hovered outside and watched Leanna hug her family good-bye.

"I love horse camp already!" Leanna announced happily as she hugged her little

sister, Sara. "Bye! See you in a week!"

Sumatra felt her lower lip tremble a bit!

"What's wrong, Sumatra?" Kona said, looking at her fellow Wind Dancer with concern.

Sumatra swallowed past the lump in her throat and stuttered, "N-nothing."

"Good!" Brisa jumped in to say. "Because you were right! Horse camp is so neat! I *love* being around all the children and big horses."

"And I love the mountain breezes!"

Sirocco chimed in, taking several deep breaths.

"And *I've* spotted a perfect place for us to stay," Kona added. "A nice soft hay pile under the eaves just outside the stables. We can sleep beneath the stars. And in the mornings, I bet the big horses will share their horse pellets with us for breakfast."

Mountain breezes? Sumatra thought. *Sleeping beneath the stars? Horse pellets?!*

"This place sure is different from home!" Sumatra couldn't help but say.

"That's the whole point, isn't it?" Sirocco said. "To be somewhere totally different? That's what you said yesterday!"

"Yes," Sumatra replied slowly. "I just didn't realize that different would feel so . . . *different.*"

Sumatra found herself thinking about all the things they'd left behind.

Just thinking about home made Sumatra feel a little sick.

A little . . . home*sick!* she realized with a start.

But clearly, Sumatra was the *only* one yearning for home.

Brisa was lounging happily on the front porch of Leanna's cabin, unconcerned, for once, about getting dirt on her pretty pink coat.

Sirocco was doing backflips in the cool mountain air.

And Kona was humming a carefree little tune as she watched Leanna and her cabin mates unpack and settle in. If the violet-black

horse was still fretting about dust or squirrel squatters back in the Wind Dancers' faraway tree house, she wasn't showing it!

What do I do now? Sumatra lamented silently. I *convinced my friends to come to horse camp. Now they love it—and I want to go home!*

CHAPTER 3
A Rotten Egg

If Sumatra wanted to go home, her chance to speak up was *now*! The pickup truck with Leanna's parents and little sister, Sara, would be leaving soon.

So, Sumatra took a deep breath and got ready to tell her friends about her change of heart. But before she could utter a sound, a crackling filled the air.

"Announcement, announcement!" sang a loud, disembodied voice. Sumatra whinnied in fright, but Sirocco's face lit up.

"Cool!" he neighed. "They're going to tell

us something on the camp intercom."

He pointed with his nose at a trumpet-shaped speaker mounted on a tree near Leanna's cabin.

"I bet we're going to hear about our first horse-camp activity!" Kona said excitedly.

Sumatra gulped.

"But," she said, "*I'd* rather—"

"Attention campers *and* horses!" A jovial voice interrupted Sumatra. "It's time to get yourselves over to the main riding ring for a little meet and greet!"

"Goody!" Brisa whinnied. She launched herself off the porch and headed for the riding ring—without even bothering to dust off her pretty coat. She was really getting into this rustic thing! Still, Sumatra tried again.

"But—"

"If your backpack's too heavy," Sirocco interrupted Sumatra, "just leave it here. We'll come back for it later."

He kicked his own backpack under a fern before flying after Brisa.

"But—" Sumatra neighed once more.

But—there was nobody left to hear her protest. Kona had darted after Brisa and Sirocco, too.

So, with a gulp and a wistful gaze toward the parking lot—where Leanna's parents and sister were cranking up their pickup truck to leave—Sumatra followed her friends.

. . .

As the campers streamed through one end

of the riding ring, several camp counselors led several big horses through the other end.

"Awesome!" Sirocco said. "Look at all those big horses!"

"They don't look anything like the big horses at *home*," Sumatra pointed out. With another pang, she imagined lanky little Andy, proud Benny, sweet Fluff, and even haughty Thelma at their neighboring big-horses paddock.

Kona only laughed.

"Of course they don't!" she said. "Every horse is unique."

"I *know* that!" Sumatra grumbled. "I just meant I miss—"

"Hellooooo campers!"

Sumatra was interrupted by a man riding a spotted gray gelding. The horse loped casually to the center of the ring.

"The first rule of horse camp," the camp director told the children, "is to *relax*. If you feel easy in your saddle, you'll ride better. You'll ride *happier*. It'll make your horse feel happy, too! And that, campers, is why I have this . . ."

He reached into his shirt pocket and pulled out a small, white—

". . . egg!" The camp director smiled as he next pulled out a large spoon and placed his delicate egg on it. Holding the spoon out before him, he chirruped to his horse, who

trotted gently
around the ring.
The egg bobbled
dangerously on the
spoon as the camp director balanced it.

"It's going to fall!" Sumatra neighed.

"And splat all over that horse's nice, shiny hooves!" Brisa added.

Somehow, though, the camp director and his big horse circled the ring without breaking the egg. The campers hooted and applauded.

"Your turn!" the camp director told the children. "And remember, if you're at all unhappy, that egg's going to fall right off that spoon!"

The campers giggled at this prospect.

"So shake out those arms and legs, and have fun!" the camp director went on.

Excitedly, the campers lined up behind the big horses. The first girl in each line was helped into her saddle, then given an egg and a spoon. The children giggled as they tried to hold the reins while at the same time balancing their wobbly, bobbly eggs. Almost immediately, eggs began falling to the dirt with *cracks, thwacks,* and *splats*!

Sumatra had to admit, the egg-in-the-spoon game *looked* like fun, but that was all. It didn't *feel* fun. Not to Sumatra anyway. She didn't feel *anything* except homesick.

Her friends, on the other hand, were completely *egg*-cited.

"*Whoo hoo!*" Sirocco laughed as the big

horses gingerly conveyed campers and eggs around the riding ring. "We've got to get in on that action!"

Brisa giggled. But Sumatra focused on the game. Or rather, on a *problem* with the game.

"We're too little to tote around those big, heavy eggs!" she pointed out.

Kona fluttered high into the air to scan the landscape.

"*A-ha!*" she called to her friends. "I see wild raspberry bushes by the lake!"

"Yum!" Sirocco said. "I could use a snack."

"They're not for eating!" admonished Kona. "We're going to carry those berries in spoons! Raspberries are just as delicate as eggs—and they're the perfect size for us!"

"Nothing's more *splatable* than a ripe, juicy raspberry!" Brisa agreed with a grin. "They'll make *perfect* 'eggs.'"

While Sirocco and Kona flew off to fetch raspberries, Brisa popped four bowl-shaped jewels out of her magic halo. She found four short twigs on the ground. Then she turned to gaze at Sumatra.

"These are my prettiest jewels yet!" Brisa said. "Now, just tie them to these sticks with your ribbons and voilà—we'll have our spoons!"

Normally, Sumatra would have jumped at this task, choosing her prettiest ribbons and tying them with fluffy bows.

But with home crowding her head, she couldn't focus on making the egg spoons. So, she only managed to pull four limp, gray ribbons out of her halo.

Then she wrapped the ribbons around the jewels and twigs, and tied them in plain old knots.

"Um, thanks," Brisa said. "I think." She gave the sad little spoons, then Sumatra, a curious look.

Brisa perked up, though, when Sirocco and Kona returned, carrying a leaf full of ripe berries!

The four horses plopped a berry each into their homemade spoons, grasped the twiggy handles in their teeth, and began flying around the riding ring.

"*Whoops!*" Brisa neighed as her berry fell to the ground. She giggled as she swooped back to the starting line to fetch another berry.

Meanwhile, Sirocco sent his berry flying with an over-eager wave of his wings. The colt guffawed good-naturedly.

When Kona dropped *her* berry, Brisa and Sirocco burst out laughing. Kona only looked stern for a moment, before her friends' infectious laughter had her nickering, too.

Only Sumatra remained stony-faced.

If I just think super-hard about this egg-on-the-spoon thing, Sumatra thought, her teeth clamped hard on her spoon's handle and her eyes squinting at her precarious berry, *maybe I* won't *think about home.*

Of course, trying *not* to think about home only made Sumatra *think* about home! And *that* caused Sumatra to hang her head sadly, which meant—

Plop!

Sumatra's raspberry fell to the dirt.

"*Ah, ha, ha!*" Sirocco crowed. "Try again, Sumatra!"

But the sad silvery blue filly just shook her head.

"We never do egg-in-spoon races at *home,*" she said. "What's the point?"

"*Fun* is the point!" Kona replied, before popping her makeshift spoon back into her mouth to give the game another try. This time, she managed to make it all the way around the riding ring with her berry intact!

"Go, Kona!" Brisa cheered.

Never one to be outdone, Sumatra gritted her teeth and tried again. But halfway around the riding ring, she heard a counselor call out, "Leanna? You're up next!"

Sumatra's muscles tensed. Leanna! Leanna was the only one—besides her fellow Wind Dancers—whom Sumatra knew in this far-away place.

Sumatra shifted her eyes to search for Leanna. But in their round, black helmets and tan breeches, all the campers looked alike! She couldn't tell which one of them was their friend.

Frustrated, Sumatra kicked the air with her hoof and—

Plop!

There went her raspberry, down in the dirt again.

"Oh, no!" Sumatra cried, spitting out her spoon and tossing her mane. "How can this be?"

"You're just a bit . . . stiff, that's all," Kona assured her filly friend.

"Well, how can I get loose when . . . when this riding ring is so big and crowded!" Sumatra blurted. "It's nothing like the big horses' cozy paddock at *home*. And don't you think these raspberries are a bit heavy? They're bigger than the ones we have at *home*."

Sumatra had one more complaint, but she couldn't bear to voice it aloud.

Clearly, I'm *better at home, too!* she told herself. *Here at horse camp? I'm too home-sick to do anything well!*

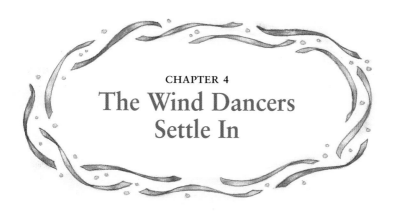

CHAPTER 4

The Wind Dancers
Settle In

Later that day, the Wind Dancers flew to the hay pile beneath the low eaves outside the horse stables.

Sumatra had just pulled her blanket from her backpack when a big horse's head poked through an open window by the hay pile.

"Hel-lo," said a chestnut mare. She had a floppy forelock and big, kind brown eyes. "Who have we here?"

Her nicker brought more curious heads through the neighboring stall windows—a golden filly and a glossy black gelding.

"Look at you teeny horses!" said the filly with a whinny. "I'm Misty. My mare friend is Flora. And this gelding is Gumdrop."

"Are you fairy-tale horses?" Gumdrop asked.

"We may be magic, but we're no fairy tale," Sirocco said proudly. "We're real, live Wind Dancers!"

"We came to horse camp with our friend, who's a camper here," Brisa went on.

"We've *never* been away from home before," Sumatra added, nuzzling her blanket for comfort.

"Oh, you'll love it!" Flora assured her. "And so do we! The girls groom us, feed us, and clean our hooves . . ."

"They even clean out our stalls!" Misty pointed out.

"Then they learn how to saddle us up and ride, ride, ride!" Flora added. "Strolling through the woods with a feather-light child on your back. There's nothing like it."

"Wouldn't it be awesome if we could carry riders, too?" Sirocco asked.

"Yeah, right," Gumdrop teased. "Even the smallest child would squash you flat!"

"And humans definitely *don't* make saddles for tiny flying horses," Flora added sympathetically.

"Well, *they* might not, but *we* can!" Kona boasted. "Right, Sumatra? You can just whip up some saddles, blankets, and bridles with your magic ribbons."

"Huh?" Sumatra said. She'd only half-heard this conversation. She'd been day-dreaming about the dandelion meadow back home.

"Saddles?" Brisa prodded Sumatra. "Trail rides?"

Sumatra blinked away her daydream—if not her homesickness—and asked, "Who would ride in our saddles?"

"Hmmm," Sirocco replied. "I know! Bugs!"

"Bugs?" Sumatra frowned. "For all we know, the insects at horse camp are twice the size of the ones at *home*. Just like the raspberries!"

"The *horseflies* sure are big!" Gumdrop agreed grouchily, swatting at a few of them with his tail

"See?!" Sumatra said.

"I'd be pleased to carry even a big bug," Brisa said, "as long as it was pretty. I bet a ladybug would match my pink coat nicely!"

"Well, you can have your chance with

riders tomorrow," Flora replied. "The campers are going on their first trail ride. They'll have a saddling lesson in the morning, then we'll all tromp up the low mountain, and then we'll have a picnic lunch."

"Ooh, we just love picnics!" Brisa said, looking to Sumatra encouragingly.

"Well, at *home* we do," Sumatra said, thinking longingly of the apple muffins and oat bars the Wind Dancers often made for their picnics. "I don't know *what* we're going to find to picnic on here!"

"Hello?" Sirocco said. "A *trail* ride calls for *trail* mix, right? We can whip some up!"

"Out of what?" Sumatra asked.

"We have some bran and barley," Misty offered.

"Too bad horses can't have nuts in their trail mix," Gumdrop added with a naughty grin. "but, you guys are *already* nuts if you think you can get bugs to ride in your saddles!"

"Hey, that's not very nice!" Kona said to the sassy gelding. "Right, Sumatra?"

"What did you say?" Sumatra murmured distractedly. Then she looked away and sighed sadly.

Her friends sighed, too.

"What can we do to make Sumatra happy again?" Brisa whispered to Kona and Sirocco. "Maybe a makeover?"

"Or some super-duper snack!" Sirocco suggested.

Kona shook her head.

"I don't think there's anything we can *do*," she said wisely. "Sumatra's joy is up to her. Hopefully, she'll have so much fun on tomorrow's trail ride that she'll stop thinking so much about home!"

CHAPTER 5

Saddled

At horse camp the next morning, Kona and Brisa flew off to see if they could rustle up some buggy riders.

Sirocco and Sumatra perched on a fence rail outside the stables to watch the campers at their lessons. The girls learned to apply halters and bridles to their horses, to lead them on ropes and rein them in, to use the stirrups to hoist themselves into their saddles, and many other horsey skills.

As Sumatra watched and learned, she weaved her colorful magic ribbons to create the Wind Dancers' tack.

She started by making four saddle pads.

"These remind me of the sleeping blankets we have at *home*," Sumatra said to herself.

Then, while she fashioned ribbons into stirrups, she asked Sirocco, "Remember how I looped ribbons *just* like this to make a soccer net back *home*?"

And as Sumatra crafted bridles, she mused, "I think I'll make these in yellow and green. Those colors remind me of our meadow filled with dandelions back *home*."

Before Sumatra could reminisce any more, Brisa and Kona returned.

"Thank goodness you're back!" Sirocco whispered. "If I have to listen to Sumatra go on about *home* for one more minute, I'm going to get homesick myself!"

"No worries," Kona said smoothly. "Soon, we're going to be too busy riding the trails to even *think* about home!"

Then she turned and said, "Come along, buggies!"

From behind a rose bush crept three adorable ladybugs and one fuzzy, black-and-yellow caterpillar.

"You ladybugs are going to look so pretty in our saddles!" Brisa added sweetly.

"Sure, for you fillies," Sirocco neighed. "But I'll take the caterpillar!"

"Now, as we agreed," Brisa reminded the insects, "in exchange for coming along for the ride, we'll give you a steady supply of snacks! Starting with . . . "

Brisa nosed around in her backpack and

emerged with three bright green blobs.

". . . aphids for the ladybugs," she said, doling out the delicacies.

"And for the caterpillar," Kona added, "I've got some tasty leaves for you to munch on!"

The insects began happily feasting. But Sumatra was less thrilled.

"You had to *pay* the bugs with food?" Sumatra balked. "I bet the bugs at *home* would have gone for the ride just to be nice!"

The caterpillar undulated its way over to one of the saddles. It plunked itself into its seat, then gave Sirocco an impatient look.

"Well, you don't get more nice than that!" Sirocco said with a happy laugh. "Help me saddle up, horses?"

The fillies nudged Sirocco's saddle blanket onto his back, followed by his saddle, caterpillar and all!

After a few more moments of buckling and tightening, the fillies were saddled up as well, each with a ladybug in their seats.

The Wind Dancers finished just in time. The campers going on the trail ride were ready to go.

"Okay, campers!" said the head counselor from her own saddle. "Since this is our first trail ride, we'll be ponying up. That means every two of you will ride with a counselor, who will have you on a lead rope. The horses know this trail, too, so they'll help you as much as you'll direct them!"

A few of the campers laughed good-naturedly at this, while the saddled big horses gazed at them with their bright, mellow eyes.

"Don't forget—there are lots of intersecting trails on the ride," the counselor went on. "We'll be following the trail marked with orange slashes on the trees. That'll take us up to the prettiest view on the mountain, where we'll have a picnic lunch!"

"Orange slashes," Kona said with a firm nod. "Got it."

"Picnic lunch!" Sirocco added, nodding proudly at the bulging bags he'd attached to either side of his saddle. "Got *that*!"

"Giddyup!" Sumatra's ladybug suddenly ordered.

Sumatra couldn't help but laugh. Her little bug may have only been doing this ride for the snacks, but she was still pretty good at playing cowgirl!

All of a sudden the idea of flying the trails with the campers (especially with a rider as entertaining as her ladybug) *did* seem fun to Sumatra.

"You know what?" she told her friends. "I think this trail ride's going to be great after all!"

"Yay!" Sirocco whinnied. Then he added, just to Brisa and to Kona, "Let's get going before Sumatra starts thinking again about ho—"

"Don't say it!" Kona interrupted with frantic looks in Sumatra's direction.

"Whoops!" Sirocco said. Then he added in a loud voice, "What I *meant* to say was, let's get going on our best trail ride ever!"

"But it's our *only* trail ride ever," Brisa noted, blinking at the colt.

"Exactly," Sirocco declared. "So it'll *have* to be our best!"

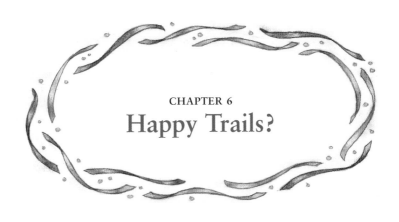

CHAPTER 6
Happy Trails?

Excitedly, the little winged horses flew over the campers making their way up the trail. The young riders were giggling so much, Sumatra almost wondered if the girls could see them. The Wind Dancers were indeed a laughable sight!

Sirocco's caterpillar, for instance, accidentally flapped its leaf snack over the colt's eyes! Unable to see for a moment, Sirocco crashed through some tree limbs and scattered branches everywhere!

Kona's ladybug pulled so much on her filly's reins that Kona found herself doing an involuntary backflip!

Brisa didn't have that problem. Her rider was so busy *nibbling* on her reins, she didn't bother to *pull* on them!

"You're a very hungry ladybug!" Brisa giggled, twisting her head around to give her pretty, black-spotted rider a nose nuzzle.

Sumatra's rider was the most unruly of all. *Her* ladybug bucked so much that Sumatra's ribbony saddle began to unravel!

"Ha!" Sumatra whinnied. She was still feeling cheery, but when her saddle and saddle blanket fell off entirely, she headed down to the trail for a landing!

"Um, horses?" Sumatra called to her friends, who quickly flew down to join her. "I think I've got a problem!"

"I'll say!" her ladybug rider said, as they landed in the dirt. "I didn't sign on to ride bareback. That's too slippery!"

"Well, maybe if you hadn't kicked so hard . . . ," Sumatra began.

"Oh, no worries," the ladybug replied smoothly, popping the last of her aphid into her mouth. "I'm done with my snack, any-way."

"Which means . . . ?" Sumatra asked tentatively.

"Which means our deal is done," the ladybug said with a shrug. "See ya, horsey!"

With that, Sumatra's rider fluttered off!

Brisa, Kona, and Sirocco gaped as the ladybug flew away.

"I bet she's flying *home,*" Sumatra suddenly lamented. And just like that, she felt her homesickness begin to return.

Which is why her friends had to act fast.

"Oh, who needs riders!" Sirocco blurted. "We can have an awesome trail ride all on our own!"

"Really?" Sumatra asked hopefully.

"Of course," Kona was quick to add. She turned to her own ladybug rider.

"Thanks so much for coming along," she told the bug. "But we can take it from here."

"Good!" the little beetle blurted. She unfurled her stiff wings and buzzed into the air. "Because I was starting to get saddle sores."

"See you!" Sirocco's caterpillar added, plopping to the ground.

"Wait for me!" Brisa's ladybug called. In a moment, she was gone, too.

Sumatra turned to her friends.

"You didn't have to send your riders away just because mine didn't work out," she protested. "Without them, you're missing out on one of the joys of horse camp!"

Kona trotted over to give Sumatra a nose nuzzle.

"We still have the big horses and campers," she said. She pointed with her nose down the trail. The last of a long line of

riders was just turning a corner, taking them out of the Wind Dancers' sight. "We also have this beautiful trail, just waiting to be discovered."

As Sumatra considered this, Brisa, Kona, and Sirocco exchanged hopeful glances. Was

Sumatra going to hang on to her newfound cheer?

The Wind Dancers sure hoped so, as they fluttered back into the air and continued down the trail.

But they moved slowly because Sirocco kept stopping to munch on trail mix.

"Colts burn a lot of energy on trail rides," he declared with his mouth full. "I've *got* to snack."

And Brisa kept getting distracted by all the pretty things she saw on the side of the trail.

"Look at those peach roses!" she exclaimed, fluttering over to give the pretty blooms a sniff.

Meanwhile, Sumatra herself was popping brightly colored ribbons out of her magic halo. She tied these ribbons with big, fluffy bows around tall-flower stems and tree branches, humming a happy tune as she went.

Suddenly, Kona realized something! "Um," she gasped, "has anyone seen the *trail* lately?"

Sumatra, Sirocco, and Brisa all gasped and looked below them. Sure enough, instead of a neat, horseshoe-tromped pathway through the trees, the Wind Dancers saw nothing but pine straw, ferns, and fallen leaves!

"We're lost?!" Sumatra neighed.

"Of course not!" Sirocco scoffed. "I'm sure the campers are close by. Let's listen!"

The Wind Dancers all cocked their ears and held their breath, straining for the sounds of big-horse nickers and campers' chatter.

But all they heard was a few birds chirping into an eerily silent forest.

"Uh-oh," Brisa murmured.

"Let's not worry yet!" Kona declared. "Remember what that counselor said? We'll just look for orange slashes on the trees."

The Wind Dancers looked.

There were no orange slashes on any of the trees around them.

All the bark was bare. Which meant . . .

"We're lost!" Brisa neighed.

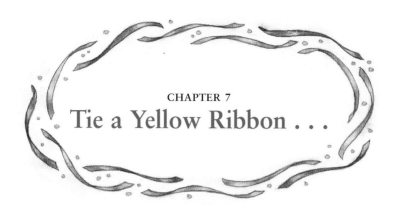

CHAPTER 7

Tie a Yellow Ribbon . . .

"I think being lost is making me a *little* upset," Brisa declared, sounding a little upset.

"It might even be making me a bit *scared*," Sirocco added, sounding a bit scared!

"And maybe for me, just a little bit homesick," Kona admitted. Her voice sounded far away, as if she was dreaming about their apple-tree house kitchen, far from these woodsy wilds.

Sumatra gazed at her fellow Wind Dancers. But instead of whinnying, weeping, or whining, too, she grinned.

"Well, now our adventure's *really* starting, isn't it?" she responded gaily.

"Okay, let me get this straight," Sirocco squawked. "*Now* you're having fun at horse camp. Now that we're lost, and cold, and *hungry?*"

"Please!" Sumatra said breezily. "We'll find our way. It's summertime, so we're not cold. And you *can't* be hungry. You've been snacking all morning!"

"True," Kona said. "But Sirocco still has a point, Sumatra. If ever there was a time at horse camp to be a bit *nervous,* this is it!"

"Right!" Brisa quavered. "I mean, there's no sign of the campers or the trail. We are as lost as lost can be!"

"Uh-huh," Sumatra muttered. She'd only been half-listening to Brisa's lament because she'd been deep in thought.

And now that her head wasn't crowded

with homesickness, her thoughts were coming clear! Which is why it took only a moment for her to open her eyes wide and blurt, "A-ha!"

"A-what?" Brisa asked glumly.

Instead of answering, Sumatra fluttered high into the air. She spun in a slow circle, squinting through the trees in every direction.

And then she saw it off in the distance—a hint of yellow! Whinnying with joy, Sumatra began flying straight toward the color.

"Where are you going?" Kona neighed.

"Follow me!" Sumatra called back over her shoulder.

For the first time since she'd convinced her friends to go to horse camp, she trusted herself!

The Wind Dancers followed Sumatra to a sapling decorated with a shiny yellow bow.

Sumatra nosed the bow with a big grin.

"I thought tying my ribbons would just make me feel at home here, make me happy," Sumatra said. "Little did I know they were also marking our path!"

Next, she pointed with her nose at a tree stump in the distance. It was bedecked with a bright green bow!

Beyond that, the peach rose bush that Brisa had admired was tied up in purple satin!

"Awesome!" Sirocco brayed.

"Oh, Sumatra!" Brisa said dramatically. "You've saved our lives!"

Kona gave her friend a very proud nose nuzzle before saying, "Come on, horses!"

Clicking their hooves and nickering with happiness, the Wind Dancers flew from bow to colorful bow until they found themselves back at the trail with the orange slashes. And before they knew it, they had followed the trail back to camp.

"Thank goodness we're back!" Sirocco said as they flew toward the stables. "I thought I'd die of starvation out there in the wilderness!"

"Oh Si-*rocco*," Brisa scoffed with a giggle. "But I agree that it's *great* to be back!"

"I'm so happy to be home, too, I could kiss the ground!" Sumatra chimed in.

Kona smiled at her.

"Home?" she joked. "Don't you mean horse camp?"

"Oh, right," Sumatra said with a chuckle. "I guess I forgot."

"*You?!* You forgot?" Sirocco neighed in triumph. "And now you think that horse camp is *home?*"

"Well," Sumatra replied with a big smile, "I feel at home here now. Why wouldn't I? I mean, the trail rides, the big horses, the campers, the mountain air—horse camp is the best thing to come around since the dandelion meadow!"

"Oh, Sumatra!" Kona laughed. "I don't know whether to give you a nose nuzzle or a hoof-clop to the head."

"I'll take the former, please," Sumatra said, as the other tiny horses crowded around her. "After all, I *did* save your lives out there on the trail!"

CHAPTER 8

Home Again,
Home Again

"Rise and shine, Wind Dancers!" Sumatra announced in the dawn's early light. "It's our last day of horse camp! We have to make the most of it!"

"Considering that we've got to be the *only* ones in camp who are already awake," Sirocco whinnied sleepily, "believe me, we'll have *plenty* of time to make the most of it!"

"There's so much to do!" Sumatra said undeterred. "Starting with eating these yummy oat cakes for breakfast!"

Sumatra pulled some delicious-looking

treats from her ribbony backpack.

"Wow!" Kona said, pricking her ears. "These sure are nicer than the horse pellets and raw oats we've been eating all week!"

"I found out where the horse trainers keep the fancy snacks!" Sumatra boasted.

"Yum-o!" Sirocco said, already munching on his oat cake, and suddenly not so sleepy.

"Eat up!" Sumatra said. "It's almost time for our final trail ride!"

"Okay, Sumatra," Sirocco answered between bites of oat cake. "We all know that you've become horse camp's trail-ride champion. There's no trail *you* can get lost on."

"Practice makes perfect!" Sumatra replied.

"And you've been practicing every single day!" Brisa said with admiration in her voice.

"Then after our ride," Sumatra went on proudly, "I have *another* activity planned for us—swimming in the lake!"

"What?" Kona said. "Sumatra, we can't swim in that deep lake!"

"I know," Sumatra said. "But the other day I took the shortcut to the dining hall . . ."

"*What* shortcut to the dining hall?" Sirocco demanded. "Sumatra, is there *anything* you don't know about horse camp?"

"No, I think I've pretty much got it covered," Sumatra joked. "Anyway, I found a super-shallow part of the lake. It's right by the shore but hidden by cattails. It'll be *so* refreshing after our trail ride."

"Speaking of refreshing," Sirocco said, "I'm kind of looking forward to napping in the back of Leanna's pickup truck on our way back home tomorrow. All these horse camp activities have worn me out!"

"And the minute we get home," Brisa added, "I'm going to soak in a long, hot bath. As much as I *love* horse camp, I'm a little tired of the hose-downs we get here."

"You're *supposed* to come home from camp feeling grimy," Kona reminded them with a smile. "*And* hungry for a home-cooked meal. Which is what I'm going to make us for dinner tomorrow!"

"Now I *really* can't wait to get home!" Sirocco whinnied.

"This week just flew by, didn't it?" Kona asked. "I can't believe it's already time to go!"

Sumatra just stared at Kona. Her eyes went wide and watery.

Then, she threw her head back and neighed, "I don't want to go home. I want to stay here at *caaaaamp*!"

"Oh, horses," Sirocco neighed between laughs. "Here we go again!"

There's No Place Like . . . Home

The next day, back home in the dandelion meadow, the Wind Dancers each soaked away their horse-camp dirt in long, hot baths (except for Sirocco, who took just a quick dip).

Then they ate a delicious Kona-cooked meal of carrot pudding, oatmeal casserole, and apple pie.

After that, they flew out into the evening. There, they hovered for a moment, enjoying the grassy scent of the dandelion meadow, the glow of fireflies, and the calm, night air.

"It's amazing how different it feels here," Sumatra commented, "compared to the breezy mountain air at horse camp."

Kona gave the filly a searching look.

"And . . ." she asked carefully, "are you okay with that?"

Sumatra cocked her head for a moment. Her coat felt clean and cool after her bath. Her belly was comfortably full of her favorite foods. And her mind brimmed with happy horse-camp memories.

So, she found herself nodding.

"I love horse camp," she admitted. "But I love home, too! I guess you *can* be happy in both places, at different times."

Kona gave Sumatra a nose nuzzle.

"You're right," she agreed. "You can."

"I wonder if Leanna is feeling the same way," Brisa said. "Or do you think she is feeling camp-sick right now?"

"There's one way to find out!" Sumatra said brightly.

The tiny horses made four beautiful silhouettes as they flew across the meadow toward Leanna's farmhouse.

When they landed on the windowsill of Leanna's room, they  found their friend in pajamas, sitting up in bed, scribbling in her pink diary. Like the Wind Dancers, Leanna looked freshly scrubbed—and happily exhausted.

She seemed so tired that she couldn't finish her journal entry. She plunked the notebook—still open—on her nightstand and snuggled down under her covers.

As soon as she turned off the lamp, she fell asleep.

Sirocco buzzed inside to take a closer peek at Leanna's diary.

"Sirocco!" Kona hissed. "You can't read

Leanna's journal. That's private!"

"Would she have left it open if she minded someone reading it?" Sirocco protested. "Besides—look! This entry is about *us*!"

The fillies pricked up their ears. They bit their lower lips. Then they gave in and joined Sirocco as he hovered above the diary.

"See," Sirocco whispered. He began to read out loud. "'Favorite things about horse camp:

1) My scrappy horse, Gumdrop, of course!

2) All my new camp friends.

3) The chocolate pudding in the dining hall. Yum!

4) Free swim at the lake . . .'

"And then:

"*I already miss horse camp so much! If I didn't know I was going back next summer, I'd be super sad!*'"

"Next summer!" Brisa exclaimed. "*Whee!*

We can go back to horse camp, too!"

Sumatra's eyes gleamed as she took over the reading from Sirocco.

"'Plus, it's nice to be back home with my family, and with my little friends, the Wind Dancers, nearby.'"

Sumatra gasped.

"Wouldn't it be fun to let her know we were here *and* there?"

"At horse camp, you mean?" Brisa asked.

Sumatra nodded. Then she picked up Leanna's pencil in her teeth, flipped to the next page in the little girl's diary and started drawing!

As she scribbled, a picture took shape—of cabins, a lake, a long, skinny horse stable, a dining hall, and, of course, horse trails, all nestled in the shadow of a pretty mountain.

"That's our horse camp!" Sirocco exclaimed. "Awesome art, Sumatra."

The silvery blue filly grinned gratefully, then turned back to her work.

The last thing that Sumatra added to her drawing were four, tiny, winged horses, darting over the heads of a cluster of helmeted girls on the trail.

Then she added a caption at the bottom of the picture: *Can't wait to go to horse camp with you again next year, Leanna!*

With that, Sumatra laid the pencil down and fluttered back out through Leanna's window. Her filly friends followed her. As the four friends flew out over the dandelion meadow, they giggled.

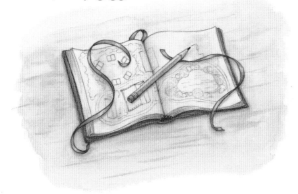

"Won't Leanna be surprised when she realizes that we shared horse camp with her!" Brisa said giddily.

Sumatra nodded happily.

"Sharing that secret is our gift to Leanna," she said. "After all, we got to go to horse camp because of her."

"Our gift might not be a necklace or a trophy this time," Kona added, recalling little presents the Wind Dancers had given Leanna in the past. "But I have the feeling Leanna will like this one just as much!"

"Me too!" Sumatra said.

With that, she led her friends back to their apple tree house, happily somersaulting and loop-de-looping all the way *home*.

Here's a sneak preview of *Wind Dancers* Book 12:

Magic Horses–or Not?

CHAPTER 1
A Big Horse Surprise

One bright morning, Kona, Sumatra, and Brisa clip-clopped into the kitchen of their apple tree house. Then the colt himself flew through the window. But instead of fluttering cheerily, his wings moved with urgency and he landed with a heavy *clunk*!

"Whoa, horsey!" Kona reprimanded him.

"It's happened!" Sirocco neighed

The fillies blinked at their friend in confusion.

"*What's* happened?" Sumatra demanded.

"Come with me and see," Sirocco said gloomily. Without another word, he flew back out the window.

The anxious fillies flew behind Sirocco as he zinged across the dandelion meadow.

He led them to Leanna's farm.

Once inside Leanna's barn, the fillies stopped in mid-air and stared!

Standing in front of a newly built stall strewn with fresh, sweet hay were Leanna and—a pony!

"Fillies," Sirocco said, unhappily, "meet Sassy, Leanna's new pet!"